ANIMAL TALES

Written by Keith Faulkner
Illustrated by Maureen Galvani

PRICE STERN SLOAN
Los Angeles

Matilda the Greedy Goat

Matilda the goat was hungry. She was always hungry. She looked around for something to eat and trotted to where the hens were pecking at some corn that the farmer had put out for them.

"Out of the way!" bleated Matilda, as she pushed all the hens aside and gobbled up the corn.

"That greedy goat!" clucked the hens.

But Matilda was still hungry, so off she trotted to the pigpen. The fat, pink pigs were all asleep, so Matilda just leaned over the low wall and gobbled up all their food, too.

"It must have been that greedy goat, Matilda!" snorted the pigs, when they woke up and found their trough empty.

Matilda went round the farm, eating everything—the cows' hay, the horses' oats, and even the cat's food!

Matilda ate everything that the other animals would eat and lots of things that they wouldn't eat. There was nothing that Matilda wouldn't eat.

"Thistles are delicious!" Matilda would say, when she saw the prickly plants that no one else would dream of eating. She also ate paper, cardboard boxes, string, old shoes, in fact, anything that happened to be lying around the farm.

Suddenly, something caught the greedy goat's eye. Just over the fence was the farmhouse and through the open window Matilda could see the farmer's favorite pie right on the kitchen table.

The fence was too high for Matilda to jump over, so she put her head down, and charged!

CRASH! The fence post snapped, as Matilda butted it with all her might, and scrambled into the garden.

By standing on her back legs, Matilda could reach the open window. One big jump and into the farmhouse kitchen she leaped.

She sniffed at the huge pie. It smelled delicious.

"Just one little nibble," thought Matilda to herself. So she took a bite. It tasted even better than it smelled. So she took another bite and then another. In a few minutes the whole pie was gone!

"Oh, no! I didn't mean to eat it all!" she said. "I can't let the farmer catch me here," said Matilda, as she tried to jump back out of the window. But because Matilda had eaten so much, she was very full, very fat, and felt very sick, so she couldn't jump at all!

"I don't feel very well," she groaned.

Just then, she heard the farmer's voice.

"I can't wait for my pie," said the farmer to his wife.

But when the farmer opened the door and looked into the kitchen all he saw was a very, very fat goat!

The farmer scolded the greedy goat. Bur poor Matilda was feeling so sick that she had learned her lesson after all!

The Rooster Who Couldn't Crow

All was silent on the farm. There was a rosy glow the early dawn sky, as the sun began to creep up over the wooded hilltop above the valley.

Just then, out of the henhouse strutted the rooster. He fluttered up onto the henhouse roof, puffed up his chest and opened his beak wide . . .

. . . but nothing came out! Certainly not a COCK-A-DOODLE-DO, as you'd expect from a rooster.

"I thought it might be different this morning," sighed the rooster, who had been trying to crow ever since he was a tiny, fluffy chick. His head hung down in shame.

All the animals laughed at him.

"He's a disgrace!" clucked the hens, as they pecked up the corn scattered in the dust.

"He can't even lay eggs," quacked the plump white ducks, swimming on the pond.

Even the farmer was upset. "If the rooster can't crow to tell me when it's dawn, how can I start work on time?" he grumbled, pulling on his heavy boots.

The next morning, the rooster was up again before dawn. He fluttered up to his favorite place on the henhouse roof.

But, just at that moment, he saw a flash of reddish fur—it was a fox, a hungry fox looking for food to steal!

The rooster gasped. "I must do something. I must warn the others. I must try to crow. I must try like I've never tried before."

So he fluffed up his feathers, took a big breath, puffed up his chest and, "COCK-A-DOODLE-DO! COCK-A-DODDLE-DO! COCK-A-DODDLE-DO!"

The rooster crowed and crowed and crowed. The farmer leaped out of his bed and threw open the curtains, just in time to see the fox race off toward the hills.

From that moment on, the rooster changed. His head didn't hang down. Instead he strutted proudly round the farmyard.

"What a hero," sighed the brown, speckled hens.

"He saved all our lives," agreed the plump white ducks on the pond.

After that, every morning as the sun creeps up over the wooded hilltop, the rooster flutters to his favorite place on the henhouse roof and greets the dawn with a very loud, "COCK-A-DOODLE-DO!"

"That old rooster's better than any alarm clock," chuckled the farmer.

The Piglet Who Wanted to See the World

The big, pink sow was very proud indeed. She had eleven fat, pink piglets. Each one had bright little eyes, a wrinkly snout, and a curly tail. And though they all looked just the same, they were not.

One of them was different. He had the same bright little eyes, wrinkly snout, and curly tail as his brothers and sisters, but he didn't act like them.

While they were happy to stay near their mother, in the warm, cozy pigpen, *he* wanted to see the world.

Everyday, the curious little piglet would stand up on his little pink back legs and gaze over the pigpen wall. One day, when the farmer came to feed them, all the little piglets fought and jostled to reach the food in the trough. But, while they were munching their meal, the little piglet trotted out of the pigpen and into the farmyard.

He looked around, wondering where to go first. He saw the open door of the henhouse and peeped inside. "Shoo! Out of here! This is our home!" clucked the hens.

So, he trotted off to the barn, but the cows began to moo loudly at him. "This is no place for you, little pig," they told him. "Off you go!"

Then the little piglet made his way into the stables, where the big hooves of the horses crashed down all around him, until he was very frightened.

"The world is a big and scary place," whimpered the little piglet to himself.

Just then, he smelled the most delicious smell. He followed it, until he reached the farmhouse. The piglet peeped into the kitchen, where on the old black stove was a tray of freshly baked cupcakes. But just as the piglet trotted into the kitchen, the farmer's wife saw him and chased him out with a broom.

The piglet ran as fast as his little feet could carry him—he ran straight back to the warm, cozy, pigpen. As he got there, the farmer was looking puzzled.

". . . eight . . . nine . . . ten," he counted. "I'm sure there were eleven piglets," he said, opening the gate to go out. Just as he did, the curious little piglet, darted in between his legs and back into the pigpen to join his brothers and sisters.

"Where have you been?" laughed the farmer. "You get back in the pigpen where you'll be safe and warm. There will be plenty of time for you to go exploring when you grow up."

But the curious little piglet didn't hear him. He had curled up in the soft, warm hay, next to his mother and was already fast asleep.

The Day the Pond Dried Up

Doris the duck dived into the pond for her morning bath. She expected a big SPLASH!, instead she landed with a thud in the wet mud.

"Where's the water?" gasped Doris, scrambling up onto the bank again.

Soon, the other ducks arrived for their morning baths. They stood and stared in amazement.

"No water!" they quacked.

"What have you done with the water?" asked Dobbin, the horse, as he came down to the pond for a drink.

"Done? Done? We haven't done anything!" cried the ducks. "It's just gone."

"It was there yesterday," said Doris. "Now it's not."

"Well I certainly didn't drink it all," said Dobbin. "Perhaps the cows did." But, the cows said they hadn't drunk it either.

"Look!" said Doris. "The stream is empty, too!" Doris was right. The little stream that usually ran into the pond was dry.

"Let's follow the stream and see if we can find the water," suggested Doris. So, they all set off up the dry stream bed. As they went along, other animals joined in the search.

But there was still no sign of any water as they made their way into Bertie the bull's field.

"Where's Bertie?" said Doris, looking for the huge bull. "I can't see him anywhere."

"I can," replied Dobbin, who was much taller than anyone else. "There he is—and there's our water!"

Bertie was lying fast asleep, right in the middle of the stream. His huge body was blocking the water completely and a big pool was slowly growing around him.

"Wake up, Bertie!" yelled Doris. "Wake up!" The huge bull groaned and opened one eye.

"Morning, Doris," he yawned. "I was having a lovely dream. It was so hot that I decided to lie in the stream to cool down. It felt very nice," he sighed.

"That wasn't a dream, silly!" said Doris. "You *are* in the stream!"

"And what's more," added the other ducks, "You've blocked it up completely!"

Bertie opened both his eyes and looked in astonishment. He scrambled to his feet and as he did, a great wave of water rushed down the dry stream bed, picking poor Doris up like a toy boat and washing her all the way back to the pond.

So, Doris got her morning bath after all!

The Monster in the Well

"But there is a monster in the well!" insisted Clara, the old hen. "I've heard it."

The other animals laughed. A monster in the well—what a stupid idea! But secretly they all thought that they'd go and look for themselves.

First, the ducks waddled over to the old well, flapped their wings and hopped up onto the edge, so they could peer down into the darkness.

"Hello!" they quacked together. Can you imagine their surprise when a voice called "Hello!" back to them!

"Clara's right!" they cried as they hurried back to the pond.

Then old Dobbin the farm horse decided to take a look.

"What nonsense!" he snorted, leaning over the well.

"What nonsense!" replied a booming voice. Poor old Dobbin galloped straight back to his stable in fright.

Big Bill, the goat, wasn't frightened of anyone. In fact, most animals were a little frightened of him.

"If there is a monster down the well, I'll give him a fright!" said Bill, as he leaned over the edge and bleated as loudly as he could.

The monster bleated back so loudly that Bill almost jumped out of his skin.

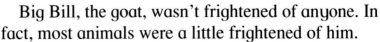

One by one, all the animals began to believe that perhaps Clara was right and there was a monster living in the old farm well after all.

"We're not going near that well," clucked the hens. "The monster might get us."

"It's not safe," agreed the ducks. "Not with a monster down there."

"Hah! How silly you all are!" laughed Claude, the rooster. "Of course there's no monster in the well. Come on, I'll prove it."

Everyone followed Claude to the well. He puffed up his chest, leaned down toward the dark hole, and went, "COCK-A-DOODLE-DO!"

As he did, an even louder "COCK-A-DOODLE-DO!" came back. The rooster turned to the animals.

"There, it's just an . . ." but before he could finish, his feet slipped and down he fell, into the well, with a SQUAWK! and a very loud SPLASH!

All the animals were horrified. They crowded round the well, trying to see what had happened to Claude, but there was no sign of him.

"Oh dear! The monster's got him," clucked the hens sadly.

But suddenly they heard a voice calling, "Help! Help! Pull me out!"

It was Claude. Quickly, everyone grabbed the rope and pulled. Slowly the bucket came up and a very wet and mad rooster appeared.

"I told you there was no monster," he spluttered. "It was just . . . an echo!"

Poor Daisy!

It was milking time. The long line of big black and white dairy cows ambled slowly across the field toward the barn.

As usual, Daisy, the little brown Jersey cow, was right at the back of the line.

"I don't know why the farmer keeps her," said Bluebell to one of the other cows.

"Just look at her," replied Cowslip. "Such a dull brown color and she's only half our size."

"Yes, he certainly can't get very much milk from her," agreed Clarabell.

Daisy was last into the barn and found the stalls were all full.

"Wait your turn," said the other cows, as the farmer began to milk them. "You know we're much more important than you are."

Poor Daisy always had to wait until last, but she never complained.

When milking was over, the farmer let the cows into the field, where there was sweet hay to eat.

"Can I have some, please?" asked Daisy, trying to push her way between the black and white cows.

"Certainly not!" snorted Clarabell. "This is our food!"

By the time the other cows had finished eating, there was no hay left for little Daisy, so she had to nibble at the grass.

Every evening the cows were led into the big barn for the night. There was straw on the floor and the barn was warm and cozy for everyone except Daisy. The other cows made her sleep by the door, where it was cold and windy. Daisy spent the night shivering.

The next day a big truck came from the dairy to collect all the milk from the farm. The cows watched from the field.

"Here it comes, girls!" shouted Cowslip. "It's the truck to collect our milk," she added proudly.

The truck pulled into the farmyard and the farmer came to help the driver load the heavy milk cans.

"You've got a lot of milk this week!" said the driver, looking at all the milk cans.

"Oh yes!" agreed the farmer. "I've got a fine herd of dairy cows! They're very good milkers!"

The cows were mooing. "Did you hear that?" said Clarabell proudly. "Good milkers! He's talking about us!"

Soon, all the cans were loaded on the truck, except one, which stood on its own.

"What about that one?" asked the driver.

"No, no, that one's not for you," replied the farmer. "That one's special. It's from my little Jersey cow, Daisy."

All the other cows turned to look at Daisy. "You see, my dear," snorted Bluebell, "your milk isn't good enough for the dairy." Then they heard the farmer speaking to the driver again.

"You can take the rest of the milk away," he explained, "but I keep the milk from Daisy just for me and my family. It's the creamiest milk in the whole world."

The big black and white cows all turned to stare at Daisy, their mouths hanging open. But Daisy just tossed her head proudly and trotted off. She didn't need to say anything.

The Cat that Wouldn't Chase Mice!

Tiger was a cat! A big cat with a striped coat, just like a tiger. He could run like the wind. He could jump and climb as well as any cat in the land.

But, he had one problem and for a farm cat, it was a very big problem indeed—he wouldn't chase mice!

Now, because Tiger didn't chase mice, all the mice liked Tiger. They came from far and wide to live on his farm, where they knew they'd be safe.

They lived in the barns, in the stables, in the pigpens, and even under the floorboards in the farmhouse.

But, the farmer was not happy with Tiger!

"That cat is useless," he said to his wife. "He has never caught a single mouse in his entire life. We'll have to get another cat—a real mouser this time!"

Some of the mice heard the farmer talking and ran to the barn to tell the others. They called a meeting and invited Tiger, too.

The barn was full of mice of different shapes, sizes, and colors and they were all squeaking loudly.

"Order! Quiet!" called the Chief Mouse. "The farmer has said that he's going to get another cat to replace Tiger. This time, a real mouser."

"Boo! Poor old Tiger!" squeaked the mice.

"You've got to do something, Tiger," said the Chief Mouse, "or you'll lose your job and we'll all be eaten."

"I've got an idea," said Tiger suddenly. "But you must help."

"We'll help, we'll help," promised all the mice.

"You must make sure that the farmer never sees you. If he doesn't see you, he'll think that you've all been chased away," Tiger told the mice.

"What are you going to do?" asked the Chief Mouse.

"Just wait and see," said Tiger, as he creeped out of the barn and headed toward the farmhouse.

Once inside, he crept upstairs and into the farmer's children's bedroom.

Tiger jumped up onto the shelf and picked up a gray, furry wind-up mouse, then he hurried quietly downstairs. As he ran through the kitchen, the farmer's wife let out a shriek.

"Oh, my goodness me! It's Tiger! He's caught a mouse!" she exclaimed.

"A mouse?" echoed the farmer. "Perhaps he's learning to catch mice. At last!"

From then on, Tiger made sure that he was carrying the wind-up mouse whenever he saw the farmer.

"Tiger is the best mouser there is," boasted the farmer to his friends. "You won't see any mice on my farm!"

The farmer was right, you would never see a mouse on the farm, but little did he know they were still there, living quietly in the barns, stables, and pigpens!

Hector to the Rescue!

As the soft white snow fell all around the farm, the animals stamped their feet and huddled together to keep warm. Even Farmer Sharples was shivering as he cleaned out the stable belonging to old Hector, the horse. Just then Mr. Turner the mail carrier drove into the farmyard.

"Morning, Mr. Sharples," said Mr. Turner, climbing out of his van with some letters. "Looks like this snow's going to get thicker before morning."

"I must get the cows in after I've cleaned up here," said the farmer, stroking Hector's nose.

"I don't know why you keep that old horse any more, now that you've got a shiny, new tractor," said Mr. Turner.

"Oh! Tractors are all right, but you can't beat a good horse," replied the farmer.

All that night the snow fell. In the morning, Farmer Sharples looked out of his window and gasped!

"Well, I never!" he exclaimed, as he saw the thick snow all round. "I must get some feed up to the sheep in the high field." Then he climbed aboard his tractor and turned the key. WHIRR! WHIRR! It wouldn't start! Farmer Sharples tried again, but the tractor didn't budge.

The snow kept falling and the farmer got more worried. His sheep up on the hillside would be cold and hungry. What could he do? He couldn't carry the heavy bales of hay. Suddenly, he heard a whinny and a stamping of hooves.

"Whoa! Hector, what's the matter?" said the farmer. "I know! You want to help."

Farmer Sharples quickly led the huge horse out.

"We've got work to do," he said, as he hitched up the sled and piled it with hay bales. "Let's go!"

As his great hooves dug into the snow, Hector heaved and off they went. The big horse ploughed through the deep snow with ease. Soon they reached the high fields and Farmer Sharples tossed off the hay bales and built a snug shelter for the sheep that were huddled on the cold hillside. Then off down the hill they went. Suddenly the farmer saw a van stuck in a deep snowdrift in the lane below them.

"Come on, Hector! Mr. Turner is in trouble."

Soon they were down beside the mail carrier's van.

"I thought I was stuck here for good," gasped Mr. Turner, shivering in the freezing wind.

"Don't worry, Hector will soon get you out," said Farmer Sharples, hitching the horse's harness to the van. "Come on, Hector! Pull!"

Hector pulled and pulled. Slowly, the van started to move, until it was clear of the snowdrift.

Mr. Turner reached into his van, flipped open his lunch box and pulled out a big, red, juicy apple.

"There you go, Hector. You deserve this," he said patting the horse's neck. "You were right, Mr. Sharples. You can't beat a good horse!"

Pirate the Champion!

Farmer Wilks' best sheepdog, Rosie, had just had five puppies. He was very pleased—and so was Rosie!

"Congratulations, Rosie!" he said, patting her head.

The little puppies were black with white patches, just like their mother. All except one! He was white, with a black patch over one eye, just like a pirate!

"I know what to call that one," laughed Farmer Wilks to himself. "I'll call him Pirate."

As the puppies grew up, old Rosie the sheepdog knew that little Pirate was going to be different. All the puppies had floppy ears, but Pirate had one floppy ear and one ear that always stood up.

"Stay with me, everyone!" Rosie would bark, as she led her puppies around the farm. "Pirate, where are you?"

Little Pirate was always somewhere he shouldn't be. He would creep into the henhouse and scare the hens. He would get in the way at milking time and annoy the cows.

"That puppy's always up to something," Farmer Wilks complained.

Rosie tried hard to keep Pirate out of trouble, but it wasn't easy. One day Pirate crept into the farmhouse and chewed up one of Farmer Wilks' best slippers!

"You bad dog!" yelled the angry farmer.

As the puppies grew up, Farmer Wilks thought it was time that they started learning how to look after the sheep.

He led Rosie and her five puppies out into the fields, where his flock were grazing.

"Go on then, Rosie, show these puppies how it's done," said Farmer Wilks.

Rosie raced off, her puppies watching her. She ran right around the field and then would lay down flat in the grass. She crept forward, until all the sheep were safely gathered together in front of the farmer.

Suddenly, one of the rams stamped his hooves and snorted. The puppies weren't used to this and they began to bark. All except Pirate.

Frightened sheep ran everywhere, but Rosie raced off to round them up again. It was then that Farmer Wilks saw one sheep running toward the open gate. Rosie would never have been able to stop it from running out into the road.

"WOOF! WOOF!" Pirate let out a bark as he saw the sheep. Then the little puppy darted off.

"Come back here, Pirate!" snorted the farmer. "You're too small for this job."

But Pirate didn't stop, he raced past the running sheep and stood in the open gateway, barking loudly, "WOOF! WOOF! WOOF! WOOF!"

The sheep stopped, took one look at Pirate standing barking in the gateway, then turned and trotted back to the flock.

Little Pirate ran back to the farmer and sat panting at his feet. Farmer Wilks reached down and patted the little dog.

"You're a funny dog, Pirate," laughed the farmer. "But I think that you're going to be the champion sheepdog one day!"

The Lamb Who Lost His Mom

"Have you seen my mom?" bleated the lamb.

"BAAA! No, we haven't," bleated the other lambs. "Come and play with us. We'll teach you how to run and jump." But the lamb didn't want to run and jump, he just wanted his mom.

He went to look in the meadow, but she wasn't there.

"Have you seen my mom?" asked the lamb, when he met some rabbits nibbling the grass down by the stream.

"We've been too busy eating," replied the rabbits. "Why don't you stay with us? We can teach you to dig holes."

But he didn't want to dig holes, he wanted to find his mom.

The little lamb wriggled through a gap in the fence and into the farmyard. There he saw some hens.

"Have you seen my mom?" he asked the hens, as they pecked in the dusty ground.

"CLUCK! CLUCK! No, no," replied the hens. "Why don't you stay with us? We can teach you to peck for corn." But the little lamb didn't want to peck for corn. He wanted to find his mom.

Near the henhouse stood a big barn. The lamb peeked inside. It was full of cows. The lamb walked in and asked the cows, "Has anyone seen my mom?"

"No, no sheep in here," the cows mooed. "Why don't you stay with us? We can teach you to MOO." But, the lost lamb didn't want to moo. So, off he trotted down to the duck pond.